To Sophie and Alice
Love from
Jill
xx

For my family with love

HARVEY AND THE MOON BUS

JILL STANTON-HUXTON

Matador
9 Priory Business Park
Wistow Road, Kibworth Beauchamp
Leicestershire. LE8 0RX
Tel: 0116 279 2299
Email: books@troubador.co.uk
Web: www.troubador.co.uk/matador
Twitter: @matadorbooks

ISBN 978 1788038 980

British Library Cataloguing in Publication Data.
A catalogue record for this book is available from the British Library.

Printed and bound by CPI Group (UK) Ltd, Croydon, CR0 4YY
Typeset in 13pt Book Antiqua by Troubador Publishing Ltd, Leicester, UK

Matador is an imprint of Troubador Publishing Ltd

Contents

Meet the Characters

Harvey

Nelly

Chester

Archie

Grey Rabbit

Gatsby

Otis and Olive

Gretel

ALL Aboard the Moon Bus

Harvey is a grey cat with big green eyes and a long bushy tail, who loves wearing his favourite pair of blue dungarees. *What a lovely sunny morning*, Harvey thought, *just the sort of day for an adventure.*

He decided to go and look for his friends: Chester, a scruffy black and white dog with pointy ears and wearing a bandana, and Nelly, a tortoiseshell cat, who never went anywhere without her multicoloured scarf wrapped around her neck. As he bounced along the front drive, Harvey saw them both heading towards the corner shop, so he ran after them.

"Chester, Nelly, wait for me!" he shouted, as they disappeared into the distance. Harvey ran as fast as he could to catch up with them and, just as he was getting out of breath, noticed them board a blue and yellow painted bus which had a sign on the front of it: 'To the Moon'. As he got closer, Harvey saw Chester and Nelly waving at him out of the window, so without a second thought he jumped on board to join them.

Harvey was surprised to see the Moon Bus driver was Archie, the old farm dog who lived

on the other side of town. "Nearly missed the Moon Bus," Archie coughed, taking off his cap and scratching the top of his head. "Just a few seats left, so sit down quickly."

"Thanks!" Harvey smiled.

"Harvey, there's a seat over there," squealed Nelly, twirling the end of her scarf in the air and pointing at a seat in the middle of the Moon Bus beside a large grey rabbit with big ears, wearing a top hat and with a big suitcase.

"Great, thanks, Nelly," he replied, rushing to sit down as the Moon Bus started to move. He noticed the grey rabbit frowned at him and mumbled something under his breath.

Harvey clicked himself into the seat belt and peered out of the window. He watched as the houses seemed to be growing smaller, which he thought was rather strange until he realised the Moon Bus was no longer on the ground but flying through the sky. The Moon Bus circled over the town then began climbing faster and higher, until finally they were in the clouds and all he could see out of the window was a thick fog.

Harvey looked around at the other passengers and noticed there were some he recognised. There was Gatsby, the old tortoise, who hibernated during the winter, and Otis and Olive, twin guinea pigs who always wore matching clothes and went everywhere together. Today they were wearing red and yellow stripey jumpers.

Harvey waved at Chester and Nelly but they were playing with a pack of cards and didn't notice him, so he unbuckled his seat belt, sat back and thought about what he might see when they landed on the Moon. He knew it had large craters on it because he'd seen some pictures of it on the television. Also, he'd heard people talk about there being cheese on the Moon – Harvey really hoped this was true because he loved cheese.

Harvey was so distracted thinking about all this that he hadn't realised the fog had now lifted outside of the window. So, when he glanced out, he had to blink several times because he couldn't believe what he was seeing – they were flying through space and it was enormous. There were lots of strange football-shaped objects floating around everywhere, which he thought must be planets. The Moon Bus was heading straight towards the nearest one, which was grey and had craters on it so he guessed it must be the Moon. Harvey was so busy looking out of the window that he jumped in his seat when he heard a loud *dinging* sound coming from the front of the Moon Bus. Harvey noticed a red sign light up, which said '*Landing Soon: Please Fasten Your Seat Belts*'.

ON the Way to Moon Crater ALLey

Harvey buckled himself into his seat belt and then noticed the grey rabbit was asleep, so Harvey tapped him on the shoulder to wake him up. He grunted several times then opened his eyes and stared across at Harvey. "We are going to be landing in a minute," Harvey said politely. The grey rabbit tutted loudly, grabbed his seat belt and buckled himself into his seat.

As the Moon Bus descended towards a large runway below, Harvey could see vehicles dashing around and a train whizzing along really fast towards a huge hangar. When they had landed, everyone collected up their belongings and started to shuffle

along the aisle towards the exit. As Harvey got nearer to the exit he could see some of the other passengers talking to Archie but he couldn't hear what they were saying. Olive was standing in front of him so he tapped her on the shoulder, "Excuse me," he whispered. "What is Archie saying to the passengers?"

"He is reminding everyone to be back at the Moon Bus by 'five o'clock sharp', otherwise he will have to leave without them," replied Olive in her squeaky voice.

Harvey was so excited about being on the Moon that he didn't worry about the fact that he couldn't tell the time. Chester could, he was really clever!

Once they were all off the Moon Bus,

Chester, Nelly and Harvey headed off towards the large hangar. "Where are we going?" he said, skipping along holding Nelly's hand.

"We're off to The Moon Rock Sweet Emporium in Moon Crater Alley," said Chester, licking his lips and wagging his tail frantically in the air.

"It's brilliant – they have all sorts of yummy flavoured sweets," Nelly laughed, letting go of Harvey's hand and twirling around in a circle.

"Oh, great – I love sweets," said Harvey, bouncing along faster than before, imagining all the tasty treats he would soon be trying.

As they reached the hangar, they could see a train on the platform with a sign on it: *'Moon Crater Alley'*.

"Quick, the doors are closing," Chester barked loudly, so they all started running as fast as they could towards the train. Harvey reached it first and just managed to hold the door open long enough for Chester and Nelly to squeeze themselves through before it shut with a loud *thud*.

"Thanks, Harvey," Nelly smiled, chewing the end of her scarf.

Before they had time to sit down the train started speeding towards a tunnel. As they all struggled to find a seat, Harvey noticed the grey rabbit, who had been sitting next to him on the Moon Bus, at the other end of the carriage.

Harvey could see that he was laughing at Gatsby, who was clinging on to his walking stick and struggling to stand upright as the train twisted and turned sharply through the tunnel. Then the grey rabbit pushed Gatsby towards one of the carriage doors. Gatsby stumbled slightly before regaining his balance and catching hold of one of the overhanging arm grips. Harvey noticed the grey rabbit was sniggering.

Harvey was just about to tell Chester and Nelly what he had seen when the train suddenly started to slow down and jolted to a stop on a platform which had a sign that read: *'Welcome to Moon Crater Alley'*.

The Moon Rock Sweet Emporium

As soon as they stepped off the train they headed down a narrow, cobbled street with shops either side of it. There were lots of displays in the shop windows to look at, but Chester and Nelly were so keen to get to The Moon Rock Sweet Emporium that Harvey couldn't slow either of them down.

The next minute they turned down a side street and there it was, in the corner of a large square, brightly lit up with coloured twinkling lights and a flashing sign hanging above the entrance. As they entered the shop, Harvey looked around and saw counters packed high with different flavoured sweets and sticks of rock. One of the counters had a sign over it that said *'Supersonic Sticky Toffee Popcorn'* and then another that said *'Raspberry Fizzy Jelly and Bubble Custard'*. He was so excited he didn't know which one to try first. While he was deciding, Chester grabbed some empty baskets and gave one to Nelly and Harvey. "Let's meet up in one hour's time by the entrance to the shop,"

said Chester, sniffing the air and licking his lips.

"Fab, fab, fab!" Nelly sang, twirling around like a ballet dancer and almost knocking into one of the counters. Before Harvey could remind them that he couldn't tell the time, they had both rushed off in different directions. He was so eager to try some of the *'Banana Marshmallow Space Sprinkles'* he'd just noticed, that he didn't think anymore about it.

Before very long, Harvey had tried lots of different flavours and his basket was full. He was just trying to find the counter with his favourite sweets – *'Strawberry Stardust Candyfloss'* (which was so chewy that it stuck

to the inside of his mouth) – when he noticed Chester and Nelly standing at the entrance looking for him. But Harvey just couldn't resist his favourite sweet so he dashed off quickly to get a few more.

A few minutes later, Harvey went to the entrance to find his friends – but they weren't there anymore, so he went outside. He stood looking amongst the busy shoppers but he couldn't see Chester and Nelly anywhere. Harvey didn't realise they had both gone into the ice-cream shop next door, thinking he might be in there. Harvey was just wondering what to do next when he spotted the grey rabbit walking briskly towards a large circus tent on the opposite side of the square. Without a second thought, Harvey decided to follow him.

He followed the grey rabbit inside the crowded tent and just managed to squeeze into a seat near the stage before the lights dimmed and loud music started to play. A spotlight appeared on the stage, and Harvey was amazed when Otis and Olive came skipping on together dressed in pink sparkly tops and bright yellow leggings. They started to climb up a long ladder, which reached all the way to the big top's roof. Once there, the guinea pigs swung back and forth together, performing all sorts of acrobatics, and making Harvey gasp with delight. After their performance, the audience stood up and clapped as Otis and Olive descended to the ground again, waved to everyone, blew squeaky kisses and skipped effortlessly off the stage.

Then the grey rabbit appeared on the stage with his top hat sat firmly on his head. The crowd watched him take off the hat, wave a wand over it – then two white doves flew out of it, disappearing over the crowd's heads. All sorts of other things appeared out of the hat after that, including a small white mouse with a long tail, dressed in a purple waistcoat with a matching cap on her head.

It was only when all the acts had finished and Harvey was outside the tent again that he remembered he should have been looking for Chester and Nelly. He was so tired though that he sat down on a nearby bench and, within seconds, fell fast asleep.

Harvey Rescues Gretel

It only felt like Harvey had been asleep for a few minutes when he was woken up by the town hall clock, in the middle of the square, chiming. He looked up at it and tried to work out the time. As he was concentrating on the clock, Harvey heard a sniffling sound coming from underneath the bench. He peered down and was surprised to see the small white mouse with the purple waistcoat that was in the grey rabbit's circus act looking back at him, with tears in her eyes.

"Are you OK?" he asked.

"No," she replied, wiping her eyes on the cuff of her jacket. "My name is Gretel and I don't like working in the circus, the grey rabbit is mean and nasty to me; he makes me perform all the time and doesn't give me much food to eat. I want to runaway, but I don't have anywhere else to go."

Harvey felt really sorry for her and wondered what he could possibly do to help. Then he had an idea. "Would you like to come home with me? There is plenty of room at my house and you wouldn't have to perform at the circus ever again."

Gretel beamed at Harvey. "Yes, thank you," she said, nibbling her fingers and curling her long tail around her tiny body, "I would love to!"

She was just about to come out from underneath the bench when suddenly the grey rabbit appeared at the entrance of the tent. Harvey noticed he pushed past an old hamster and nearly knocked him over. Gretel let out a tiny squeal when she saw the grey rabbit heading towards her. She curled herself up into a small ball and wrapped her tail around her as tightly as possible. Harvey quickly scooped her up in his paws and felt her trembling. He emptied the top pocket of his dungarees of all the sweets, stuffed as many as he could in his side pockets then placed Gretel carefully inside. "Don't make a noise, Gretel. You will be safe with me," he whispered.

Meanwhile the grey rabbit was scurrying around in all the bushes looking for her.

"You seen a small white mouse with a purple jacket on?" he snapped at Harvey as he continued to look in the bushes.

"No," Harvey replied in his bravest voice.

The grey rabbit stopped in his tracks and

stared directly at Harvey. "You sure about that?" he quizzed.

Harvey felt his heart pounding and took a deep breath. "Absolutely sure," he replied as calmly as he could.

With a shrug the grey rabbit continued his search until eventually he gave up looking, huffed and puffed, shook his head several times and then headed back inside the tent.

Harvey opened the pocket of his dungarees and quietly said, "It's OK, Gretel, you are safe now."

She slowly uncurled herself and peered over the top of the pocket.

"Thank you for rescuing me," she replied softly.

Harvey suddenly remembered that they must get back to the Moon Bus before it set off home again, otherwise they would both be left on the Moon for the night with nowhere to go. He looked up at the town clock again and sighed loudly.

"What's the matter?" asked Gretel.

"I can't tell the time," he mumbled, embarrassed, pointing to the town hall clock and rubbing his eyes.

Gretel looked across at it. "It's 4.45pm," she replied.

"Oh, no," Harvey screeched, "we only have fifteen minutes to get back to the Moon Bus – otherwise it will leave without us." Gretel noticed his whiskers were twitching uncontrollably. "I've no idea where my friends are, and I don't know the way back without them. What are we going to do?"

THe HeLter SKeLter aNd tHe Magic Mat

"It's OK," smiled Gretel, fiddling with the buttons on her jacket. "The Helter Skelter, on the other side of the square, will help us! It has magic mats which can take you anywhere on the Moon that you want to go, and it's really quick." Gretel looked up at Harvey and continued, "I've often watched the magic mats whizzing off in all directions with passengers holding on as tight as they can."

"Brilliant," Harvey said and, without a second to lose, he ran as fast as he could to the Helter Skelter. He was short of breath when he reached the top and was surprised to find Gatsby, the old tortoise, carefully placing a magic mat down on the slide and two young hamsters jumping on to it.

"Remember what I told you," said Gatsby,

looking at them, "hold on tightly." The next moment there was a loud *whooshing* noise and the magic mat took off down the slide.

As he put the next magic mat down slowly on the slide, Gatsby looked at them both, "What are you two young rascals up to then?"

"I'm taking Gretel home with me as she doesn't like working in the circus, the grey rabbit is horrid to her," Harvey said proudly.

Gretel nodded in agreement at Gatsby.

"He's a nasty piece of work, that grey rabbit," Gatsby agreed, brushing the magic mat over with a broom. "Well done for rescuing young Gretel," he continued, as he put the broom down and patted Harvey on the head. "Now on you both get. Hold on tight, Harvey, and, Gretel, you stay safely in his pocket."

"What do we do now?" said Harvey as he sat down on the magic mat.

"Tell the magic mat where you want to go and it will take you there the quickest way possible. Oh, and you have three wishes in total should you need them," said Gatsby as he moved away from the slide.

"Thank you for your help," smiled Harvey. Then in his loudest voice he made his first wish and bellowed, "I wish the magic mat would take us, as quickly as possible, to the Moon Bus."

For a few seconds nothing happened, and then suddenly the magic mat started sliding down the Helter Skelter. It got faster and faster as it headed down the slide and then magically lifted off the ground and flew upwards into the air. It took a sharp left turn over the square and headed straight towards the entrance to a huge crater in the distance.

Harvey looked below at the crowded winding streets he had walked up earlier with Chester and Nelly. Then he spotted them both heading for the train station. They were rushing along as fast as they could and not far behind them was the grey rabbit, dragging his big suitcase behind him and pushing his way through the crowds.

Harvey was so busy watching the grey rabbit that he hadn't realised they were near the entrance to the crater until everything suddenly went dark. It took a few seconds for his eyes to adjust to the darkness before he looked down below and saw the twinkling lights of tiny houses.

Harvey could feel Gretel fidgeting in his pocket so he took one of his paws off the magic mat and opened it to check that she was OK. Gretel poked her head out and looked below at the twinkling lights. They were both so mesmerised that they didn't

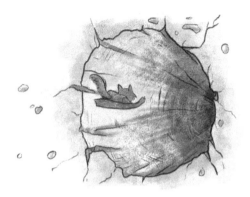

notice a small tunnel ahead of them. The magic mat slowed down, tilted slightly and Gretel fell out of Harvey's pocket and plummeted towards the ground.

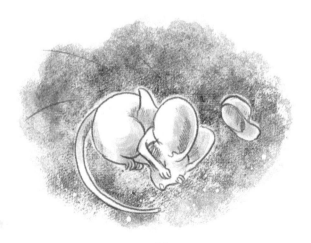

THe MooN BuS iS AbouT to TaKe OFF

"Oh, no, Gretel!" Harvey shouted as he watched her falling uncontrollably towards the twinkling lights. He tried desperately to turn the magic mat around but it continued on its journey. In desperation he tried jumping up and down on it to try and make it go slower, but nothing happened. And then he remembered the wishes: Gatsby had said he had three wishes in total, so he still had two wishes left.

Without a moment to waste, he made his second wish, that the magic mat would fly down and catch Gretel safely. The magic mat came to an abrupt halt, turned around and headed straight towards Gretel, who was now a tiny speck in the distance. Amazingly, within seconds the magic mat had reached her.

"Quick, grab my paw," Harvey shouted, as he held it out to her. She was spinning and tumbling, faster and faster out of control, but managed to wrap her long tail around Harvey's paw and he pulled her safely back onto the magic mat. He grabbed her trembling little body and lifted her back into

the pocket of his dungarees. She instantly popped her head out of the top and clung on as tightly as she could.

The magic mat turned itself around sharply again and headed back to the small tunnel entrance. They entered the tunnel and were in complete darkness. Harvey could see a faint light in the distance, which the magic mat was whizzing its way towards. Seconds later they were out of the tunnel and they could see the Moon Bus on the runway – it was just about to take off!

Harvey knew straight away what he had to do – he made his third and final wish for the magic mat to catch up with the Moon Bus as it picked up speed along the runway. Moments later they were flying alongside it.

Gretel looked up at Harvey. "The Moon Bus driver hasn't seen us," she squealed.

Harvey wasn't sure what to do, and then Chester and Nelly noticed them from the inside of the Moon Bus and they started shouting something, which made the other passengers look out of the window at them. Suddenly, Archie the Moon Bus driver saw what was happening, and he pressed a button underneath the steering wheel and the door of the Moon Bus opened.

"Jump on board, now!" he shouted.

Gretel quickly curled herself up into a tight ball inside Harvey's pocket and he took a giant leap and landed on the floor beside Archie.

"Take a seat and buckle up as quickly as possible," instructed Archie, putting his foot firmly on the accelerator pedal.

"Harvey, you can squeeze in between us," shouted Chester and Nelly, waving frantically from the back of the Moon Bus.

Harvey dusted himself down, checked Gretel was OK and then rushed towards his friends.

"Oh, Harvey, thank goodness you are OK! We looked for you everywhere?" Nelly said, sucking the end of her scarf.

"Yes, what happened to you? We've been really worried," Chester said, scratching the back of his ear.

Before Harvey could answer them, Gretel

let out a loud cry and pointed outside the window. They all turned to see what she was pointing at and saw the grey rabbit running along the runway desperately trying to catch up with them. Harvey could see that Archie

had noticed him, but he just tutted loudly, as the Moon Bus finally lifted off the runway and climbed higher and higher until they were finally in space.

Harvey let out a loud sigh of relief and Gretel tucked herself back inside his pocket for a well-deserved sleep. Chester and Nelly snuggled up close to Harvey, waiting eagerly to hear about the exciting things that had happened to him. But Harvey suddenly felt very tired so he closed his eyes and,

within seconds, was fast asleep, happily
dreaming about The Moon Rock Sweet
Emporium and his fantastic adventure on
the Moon.

About the Author

Jill has a BA Honours Degree, a Diploma in Humanities and a Diploma in Literature & Creative Writing from the Open University. She has had non-fiction articles, short stories and poems published in magazines, local newspapers and online. She was also the winner of The Buckinghamshire Family History Society Alan Dell Memorial Award for 2013.

The inspiration for the book came from Jill and her husband's beautiful and charismatic Norwegian Forest Cat, Macavity. He is now six years old and has become a local celebrity.

Harvey and the Moon Bus is her debut children's book and is the first in a planned series of Harvey books.

www.facebook.com/Jill-Stanton-Huxton

www.facebook.com/Harvey-and-the-Moon-Bus

Twitter: JMStantonHuxton

Emily Brady is a cartoonist and illustrator and her work can be found at

www.footloosecomic.com